This Book Belongs To:

MOTHER GOOSE
RHYMES AND RIDDLES

Designed and Illustrated
By Myron and Tracy McVay

♔ Hallmark Children's Editions

MOTHER GOOSE
RHYMES AND RIDDLES

Here we go round the mulberry bush,
The mulberry bush, the mulberry bush,
Here we go round the mulberry bush,
On a cold and frosty morning.

This is the way we wash our hands,
Wash our hands, wash our hands,
This is the way we wash our hands,
On a cold and frosty morning.

This is the way we wash our clothes,
Wash our clothes, wash our clothes,
This is the way we wash our clothes,
On a cold and frosty morning.

This is the way we go to school,
Go to school, go to school,
This is the way we go to school,
On a cold and frosty morning.

Little Robin Redbreast sat upon a tree,
Up went pussy cat, and down went he;
Down came pussy, and away Robin ran;
Says little Robin Redbreast, Catch me if you can.

Little Robin Redbreast jumped upon a wall,
Pussy cat jumped after him, and almost got a fall;
Little Robin chirped and sang, and what did pussy
    say?
Pussy cat said, Mew, and Robin jumped away.

Monday's child is fair of face,
Tuesday's child is full of grace,
Wednesday's child is full of woe,
Thursday's child has far to go,
Friday's child is loving and giving,
Saturday's child works hard for its living;
But the child that is born on the Sabbath day
Is bonny and blithe and good and gay.

Tweedledum and Tweedledee
    Agreed to have a battle,
For Tweedledum said Tweedledee
Had spoiled his nice new rattle.
Just then flew by a monstrous crow,
    As big as a tar-barrel,
Which frightened both the heroes so,
    They quite forgot their quarrel.

Two little dicky birds
Sitting on a wall,
One named Peter,
The other named Paul.
Fly away, Peter!
Fly away, Paul!
Come back, Peter!
Come back, Paul!

Diddle, diddle, dumpling, my son John,
Went to bed with his trousers on;
One shoe off, and one shoe on,
Diddle, diddle, dumpling, my son John.

Cock a doodle doo!
My dame has lost her shoe,
My master's lost his fiddlestick,
And knows not what to do.

There was a crooked man,
  And he walked a crooked mile,
He found a crooked sixpence
  Against a crooked stile;
He bought a crooked cat,
  Which caught a crooked mouse,
And they all lived together
  In a little crooked house.

Hot cross buns!
Hot cross buns!
One a penny, two a penny,
Hot cross buns!

If your daughters do not like them
Give them to your sons;
But if you haven't any of these pretty little
   elves
You cannot do better than eat them yourselves.

Bell horses, bell horses,
    What time of day?
One o'clock, two o'clock,
    Three and away.

One to make ready,
    And two to prepare;
Good luck to the rider,
    And away goes the mare.

One for the money,
    Two for the show,
Three to make ready,
    And four to go.

One, Two — buckle my shoe;
Three, Four — open the door;
Five, Six — pick up sticks;
Seven, Eight — lay them straight;
Nine, Ten — a big fat hen.

Peter, Peter, pumpkin eater,
Had a wife and couldn't keep her;
He put her in a pumpkin shell,
And then he kept her very well.

Intery, mintery, cutery, corn,
Apple seed and briar thorn,
Wire, briar, limber lock,
Five geese in a flock,
Sit and sing by a spring,
O-U-T, and in again.

Oh where, oh where has my little dog gone?
    Oh where, oh where can he be?
With his ears cut short and his tail cut long,
    Oh where, oh where is he?

Little Nancy Etticoat
With a white petticoat,
    And a red nose;
She has no feet or hands,
The longer she stands
    The shorter she grows.

[*A lighted candle*

Betty Botter bought some butter,
But, she said, the butter's bitter;
If I put it in my batter
It will make my batter bitter;
But a bit of better butter,
Will make my batter better.
So she bought a bit of butter
Better than her bitter butter,
And she put it in her batter
And the batter was not bitter.
So 'twas better Betty Botter bought a bit
    of better butter.

One misty, moisty morning,
When cloudy was the weather,
I chanced to meet an old man clothed all in
    leather.
He began to compliment, and I began to grin,
How do you do, and how do you do?
And how do you do again?

Sing a song of sixpence,
    A pocket full of rye;
Four and twenty blackbirds,
    Baked in a pie.

When the pie was opened,
    The birds began to sing;
Was not that a dainty dish,
    To set before the king?

Here am I,
Little Jumping Joan;
When nobody's with me
I'm all alone.

Three young rats with black felt hats,
Three young ducks with white straw flats,
Three young dogs with curling tails,
Three young cats with demi-veils,
Went out to walk with two young pigs
In satin vests and sorrel wigs;
But suddenly it chanced to rain
And so they all went home again.

The north wind doth blow,
And we shall have snow,
And what will poor robin do then?
    Poor Thing.
He'll sit in a barn,
And keep himself warm,
And hide his head under his wing.
    Poor Thing.

Old King Cole
    Was a merry old soul,
And a merry old soul was he;
    He called for his pipe,
        And he called for his bowl,
And he called for his fiddlers three.

Bow-wow, says the dog;
　　Mew-mew, says the cat;
Grunt, grunt, goes the hog;
　　And squeak, goes the rat.
Tu-whu, says the owl;
　　Caw, caw, says the crow;
Quack, quack, says the duck;
　　And what cuckoos say you know.
So with sparrows and owls,
　　With rats and with dogs,
With ducks and with crows,
　　With cats and with hogs,
A fine song I have made,
　　To please you, my dear;
And if it's well sung,
　　'Twill be charming to hear.

Daffy-down-dilly is new come to town,
With a yellow petticoat, and a green gown.
　　　　[*A daffodil*

The waves never sleep —
By night and by day
They leap and they dance,
They tumble and play,
And sing a sweet song;
But what do they say?

To market, to market, to buy a fat pig,
Home again, home again, jiggety-jig;
To market, to market, to buy a fat hog,
Home again, home again, jiggety-jog.

Hey diddle diddle,
The cat and the fiddle,
The cow jumped over the moon;
The little dog laughed
To see such sport
And the dish ran away with the spoon.

Thirty days hath September,
April, June, and November;
All the rest have thirty-one,
Excepting February alone,
And that has twenty-eight days clear
And twenty-nine in each leap year.

Oh do you know the Muffin Man
Who lives in Drury Lane?
Oh yes I know the Muffin Man
Who lives in Drury Lane.

Jack be nimble,
Jack be quick,
Jack jump over
The candle stick.

Christmas is coming, the geese are getting fat,
Please to put a penny in an old man's hat;
If you haven't got a penny
A ha'penny will do,
If you haven't got a ha'penny,
Then God bless you!

Little Robin Redbreast
    Sat upon a rail;
Niddle noddle went his head,
    Wiggle waggle went his tail.

A farmer went trotting upon his grey mare,
    Bumpety, bumpety, bump!
With his daughter behind him so rosy and fair,
    Lumpety, lumpety, lump!

Once I saw a little bird
    Come hop, hop, hop,
And I cried, Little bird,
    Will you stop, stop, stop?
I was going to the window
    To say, How do you do?
But he shook his little tail,
    And away he flew.

Humpty Dumpty sat on a wall,
Humpty Dumpty had a great fall;
　　All the king's horses,
　　And all the king's men,
Couldn't put Humpty Dumpty together again.

I saw a fishpond all on fire
I saw a house bow to a squire
I saw a parson twelve feet high
I saw a cottage near the sky
I saw a balloon made of lead
I saw a coffin drop down dead
I saw two sparrows run a race
I saw two horses making lace
I saw a girl just like a cat
I saw a kitten wear a hat
I saw a man who saw these too
And said though strange
    they all were true.

Hickety, pickety, my black hen,
She lays eggs for gentlemen;
Sometimes nine and sometimes ten,
Hickety, pickety, my black hen.

Bow, wow, wow,
Whose dog art thou?
Little Tom Tinker's dog,
Bow, wow, wow.

Dickery, dickery, dare,
The pig flew up in the air;
The man in brown soon brought him down,
Dickery, dickery, dare.

In marble halls as white as milk,
Lined with a skin as soft as silk,
Within a fountain crystal-clear,
A golden apple doth appear.
No doors there are to this stronghold,
Yet thieves break in and steal the gold.

[*An egg*

Old Mother Goose,
  When she wanted to wander,
Would ride through the air
  On a very fine gander.

See-saw, sacradown,
Which is the way to London town?
One foot up and the other foot down,
That is the way to London town.

Here sits the Lord Mayor,
  Here sit his men,
Here sits the cockadoodle,
  Here sits the hen,
Here sit the little chickens,
  Here they run in,
Chin chopper, chin chopper,
  Chin chopper, chin!

[*A child's face*

29

See-saw, Margery Daw,
Jacky shall have a new master;
Jacky shall have but a penny a day
Because he can't work any faster.

Donkey, donkey, old and gray,
Open your mouth and gently bray;
Lift your ears and blow your horn,
To wake the world this sleepy morn.

Pease-porridge hot,
Pease-porridge cold,
Pease-porridge in the pot
Nine days old.
Some like it hot,
Some like it cold,
Some like it in the pot
Nine days old.

Wee Willie Winkie runs through the town,
Upstairs and downstairs in his nightgown,
Rapping at the window, crying through the lock,
Are the children all in bed, for now it's eight
o'clock?

A swarm of bees in May
Is worth a load of hay;
A swarm of bees in June
Is worth a silver spoon;
A swarm of bees in July
Is not worth a fly.

Three wise men of Gotham
Went to sea in a bowl,
And if the bowl had been stronger
My story would have been longer.

What's the news of the day,
Good neighbor, I pray?
They say the balloon
Has gone up to the moon.

As I was going to St. Ives
I met a man with seven wives.
Each wife had seven sacks,
Each sack had seven cats,
Each cat had seven kits:
    Kits, cats, sacks and wives,
    How many were going to St. Ives?
            [One

Knock on the door,
Peek in,
Lift up the latch,
Walk in.

Ring-a-ring o' roses,
A pocket full of posies;
A-tishoo! A-tishoo!
We all fall down.

Butterfly, butterfly, whence do you come?
I know not; I ask not; I never had home.

Butterfly, butterfly, where do you go?
Where the sun shines, and where the buds grow.

Pat-a-cake, pat-a-cake, baker's man,
Bake me a cake as fast as you can;
Pat it and prick it, and mark it with B,
Put it in the oven for baby and me.

If all the seas were one sea,
What a *great* sea that would be!
And if all the trees were one tree,
What a *great* tree that would be!
And if all the axes were one axe,
What a *great* axe that would be!
And if all the men were one man,
What a *great* man he would be!
And if the *great* man took the *great* axe,
And cut down the *great* tree,
And let it fall into the *great* sea,
What a splish-splash that would be!

Doctor Foster went to Gloucester
In a shower of rain;
He stepped in a puddle,
Right up to his middle,
And never went there again.

T his little pig went to market,

This little pig stayed at home,

This little pig had roast beef,

This little pig had none,

And this little pig cried,
Wee-wee-wee-wee-wee,
I can't find my way home.

Old Mother Twitchett has but one eye,
And a long tail which she can let fly,
And every time she goes over a gap,
She leaves a bit of her tail in a trap.

[*A needle and thread*

Old chairs to mend! Old chairs to mend!
I never would cry old chairs to mend,
If I'd as much money as I could spend,
I never would cry old chairs to mend.

Thirty white horses upon a red hill,
Now they tramp,
Now they champ,
Now they stand still.

[*Teeth*

Dance, little baby, dance up high!
Never mind, baby, mother is by.
Crow and caper, caper and crow,
There, little baby, there you go!

Elizabeth, Elspeth, Betsy, and Bess,
They all went together to seek a bird's nest;
They found a bird's nest with five eggs in,
They all took one, and left four in.

There was a man in our town,
    And he was wondrous wise;
He jumped into a bramble-bush,
    And scratched out both his eyes;
And when he saw his eyes were out,
    With all his might and main,
He jumped into another bush
    And scratched them in again.

Ride a cock-horse to Banbury Cross,
To see a fine lady upon a white horse;
Rings on her fingers and bells on her toes,
And she shall have music wherever she goes.

Jeremiah, blow the fire,
    Puff, puff, puff!
First you blow it gently,
    Then you blow it rough.

There was an old woman
Lived under a hill,
And if she's not gone
She lives there still.

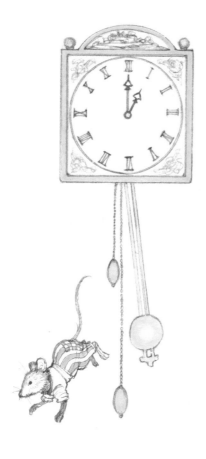

Hickory, dickory, dock,
The mouse ran up the clock.
The clock struck one,
The mouse ran down,
Hickory, dickory, dock.

Lavender's blue
Diddle, diddle,
Lavender's green;
When I am king
Diddle, diddle,
You shall be queen.

A wise old owl lived in an oak;
The more he saw the less he spoke;
The less he spoke the more he heard.
Why aren't we all like that wise old bird?

Peter Piper picked a peck of pickled pepper;
A peck of pickled pepper Peter Piper picked.
If Peter Piper picked a peck of pickled pepper,
Where's the peck of pickled pepper
Peter Piper picked?

Cackle, cackle, Mother Goose,
Have you any feathers loose?
Truly have I, pretty fellow,
Half enough to fill a pillow.
Here are quills, take one or two,
And down to make a bed for you.

Index of First Lines

Set in Goudy Old Style,
a typeface designed by Frederic W. Goudy,
first issued by American Typefounders, 1914-1915.
Printed on Hallmark Eggshell Book paper.

J